Siamese
Cats

BY NANCY FURSTINGER

Published by The Child's World®
1980 Lookout Drive • Mankato, MN 56003-1705
800-599-READ • www.childsworld.com

Acknowledgments
The Child's World®: Mary Berendes, Publishing Director
Red Line Editorial: Editorial direction
The Design Lab: Design
Amnet: Production
Design elements: Krissi Lundgren/iStockphoto; iStockphoto; Brooke
Becker/Shutterstock Images; Shutterstock Images; Willem Havenaar/
Shutterstock Images

Photographs ©: Krissi Lundgren/iStockphoto, cover, 1, 23;
iStockphoto, cover, 1, 5, 11, 14; Brooke Becker/Shutterstock
Images, cover, 1; Shutterstock Images, cover, 1; Willem Havenaar/
Shutterstock Images, cover, 1; Luca Tettoni/Robert Harding/
Newscom, 7; Henk Badenhorst/iStockphoto, 9; Ivonne Wierink/
Shutterstock Images, 13; Walt Disney Productions/Album/Newscom,
17; Fuse/Thinkstock, 19; Maslov Dmitry/Shutterstock Images, 21

ISBN 9781626873872
LCCN 2014930643

Printed in the United States of America
Mankato, MN
July, 2014
PA02226

ABOUT THE AUTHOR

Nancy Furstinger has been speaking up for animals since she learned to talk. She is the author of nearly 100 books, including many on her favorite topic: animals! She shares her home with big dogs and house rabbits.

CONTENTS

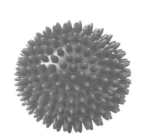

Tame Wild Cats

Siamese cats are one of the most popular cat **breeds**. This smart and loving animal is very playful. Siamese enjoy playing with toys and doing tricks. They make good pets for the right people. Their owners must enjoy having fun as well.

Some cats are made up of round shapes. Siamese are made up of long lines and angles. These cats look very noble. They are long and sleek.

Siamese cats are very vocal. However, they won't roar like some of their bigger wild cousins such as the lion. But Siamese will grab **prey** the same way a wild cat would.

Today there are 600 million house cats around the world. Cats in the United States belong to one of 42 different breeds. Siamese is one of these breeds.

These cats attract attention with their sleek coats and bright blue eyes. Their coats come in four different color patterns.

Siamese cats love attention and enjoy being around people.

Royal Cats

The Siamese breed started in eastern Asia. Many stories say this breed came from Thailand. This country used to be called Siam. Siamese cats lived in the palace with the king of Siam. They were known as the royal cats of Siam. They also lived in Buddhist temples.

The people of Siam told many stories about their cats. One story tells of a pet cat that guarded rings belonging to the royal princess. The cat kept the rings safe by wearing them on his tail. Some Siamese cats had a kink in their tails. The kink at the end of the cat's tail kept the rings from sliding off.

Another story tells of two cats living with a monk. These cats guarded a royal goblet. One day the monk left the temple. The male cat went out to find a new monk. The female stayed behind. She twisted her tail around the goblet. No one could steal it as she slept. The male returned and found the female had a kink in her tail from the goblet.

The cat that guarded the goblet gave birth to kittens. They also had kinks in their tails!

Drawings of Siamese cats also appeared in books. The book *Cat Book Poems* was written in Siam around 1350. It shows a creamy cat with a brown mask, ears, feet, and tail.

Siamese cats have appeared in books since the 1300s, including this Thai book from 1902.

Nightmare Cats

Siamese cats traveled west in the 1880s. The king of Siam gave two of his cats to a British official. The official took the cats back to Great Britain. The cats had kittens. They participated in a London cat show in 1885.

The first cats from Siam did not look like today's Siamese cats. They had **stocky** bodies. Their tails had a kink and some were cross-eyed. These Siamese cats had round heads. They were called "appleheads." Many people in Britain thought the cats looked strange. They described them as a "nightmare kind of cat."

These strange-looking cats charmed many people. One Siamese cat lived in the White House. His name was Siam. He was the pet of President Rutherford B. Hayes and his wife. Siam helped make the breed more popular in the United States.

Lean cats with more angles started to become popular in the 1900s. People thought these noble cats were more eye-catching. It wasn't long before the Siamese cat became the third most popular shorthaired cat in the United States. The Cat Fanciers' Association (CFA) recognized the Siamese starting in 1934.

The Siamese breed gained popularity in the United States in the 1900s for their special looks.

Long and Sleek

Siamese are medium-sized cats. Males can weigh between 8 and 12 pounds (4 and 5 kg). Females are smaller. They weigh between 6 and 8 pounds (3 and 4 kg).

The Siamese is now prized for its striking looks. The modern Siamese is nicknamed the wedgehead. It looks very different from its older cousins. Modern Siamese cats are long and slender. They no longer have round stocky features. Siamese have many angles. Their head is long and shaped like a triangle. Their ears are also triangle shaped. The legs and tail are long. Their body is shaped like a long tube.

Siamese cats have short hair. The fur lies close to the cat's body. Their fur is sleek and glossy.

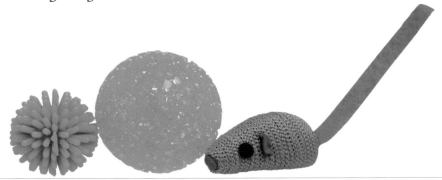

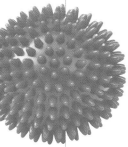

Siamese have eyes shaped like almonds. The eyes are angled down toward the nose. They slant up toward the ears. All cats of this breed have bright blue eyes.

Purebred Siamese cats will always have blue eyes.

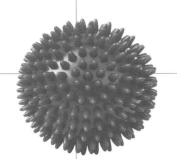

Pointed Coats

Siamese cats have darker areas on their fur called **points**. This dark fur makes a mask on their faces. It covers their ears. Their tails and legs also look like they were dipped in a dark color. The points stand out against the cats' light brown or white coats.

Points come in four colors. The first cats from Siam had seal points. This dark brown color is the darkest of the four colors. Chocolate points look like chocolate candy. Blue points are slate gray. Lilac points are a silver color.

The shade of the points depends on **climate**. Cats that live in warm spots have lighter points. Even cats that live in cold spots but like to snooze in the sun can have light points. Cats that stay out of the sun or live where it is cold have dark points. Points grow darker with age.

All litters of Siamese kittens have white coats. The color points take about one year to form.

Seal points are the darkest color and were seen on the first Siamese cats.

Lively and Noisy

Siamese cats are full of energy. They like to play with their owners. These cats demand to be noticed. Some sneak into laps. Others prefer to stretch across shoulders. They seem to want love. They usually bond with one special human.

Siamese cats are smart. Kittens are clever at an early age. They are bold and act like grown-up cats. Siamese often beat other cats when it comes to learning tricks. These smart cats can be taught to play fetch or answer to a whistle. They will even come up with new tricks on their own, such as opening the refrigerator!

Kittens and adults seek out warmth. They pile up in heaps. They take catnaps in sunny spots. They snuggle under covers.

This breed is very **vocal**. Siamese cats have loud voices. They sound like they are talking. Their meow can be mistaken for a baby crying!

Siamese use all 16 of their voice patterns. They hiss and growl. They meow and yowl.

Siamese cats enjoy snuggling in blankets and other warm places.

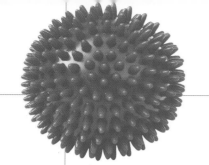

Famous Felines

Siamese have movie star looks. They star in many movies. They have energy to spare so they make great animal actors!

Two Siamese cats named Si and Am appear in the 1955 animated movie *Lady and the Tramp*. These naughty cats cause trouble. Si and Am blame everything on a dog named Lady.

A Siamese cat stars in the popular Skippyjon Jones book series. This kitten was inspired by author/illustrator Judy Schachner's own cat, Skippy. Skippyjon has such big ears that he daydreams he's a chihuahua! The cat hero has adventures around the world and in outer space.

In the 1963 movie *The Incredible Journey*, a cat and two dogs take a big trip. They travel 300 miles (483 km) through Canada to get home. Tao the cat helps the dogs survive. This seal-point Siamese opens doors. He hunts for food. He hates other cats but loves his dog pals!

A Siamese cat stars in the 1965 movie *That Darn Cat!* **Tomcat** DC holds the clue to a crime. He keeps the FBI running in circles all through this hit movie.

Si and Am cause a lot of trouble in the Disney movie, *Lady and the Tramp*.

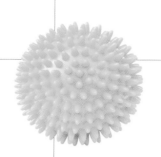

Cat Care

Siamese are known as a healthy breed. They can live 15 years or longer. Cats need to visit **veterinarians**. This helps keep them healthy. Veterinarians check the cats all over and then give them **vaccines**.

Siamese cats should be kept indoors. This is the safest spot for them to live. Cat supplies help them feel at home. Cats need beds to take catnaps. They need crates for trips. They need bowls for food and water. And they need litter boxes where they can go to the bathroom.

Cats also need scratching posts. They quickly learn to sharpen their claws on posts. This keeps them from ruining furniture and carpets.

Siamese cats are easy to groom. Their short coats do not **mat**. But they do shed. Siamese do most of the work. They use their rough tongues as combs. They still need to be groomed with a brush every week. This will get rid of loose fur. They also need to have their nails trimmed.

It is important to take your cat to the veterinarian to help keep it healthy.

Fun-Seeking Cats

Siamese cats like a wide range of toys. They will play with toys for hours. They choose their favorites. Kittens will play with their top toys for their entire lives.

These cats love a game of fetch. They will chase balls and toys that people throw. Then they will bring back the item to the person who threw it. They will return it to the person's lap!

Siamese are curious cats. They are eager to get involved in everything. This breed has a close friendship with its family. They like to follow them everywhere. They will join the family for outside walks on a leash.

Most Siamese do not like being alone. They like to play with other cats. This way they can amuse each other! Then they can live a long and happy life together.

Siamese can act like dogs. They show off their smarts by doing tricks. They also enjoy games of hide-and-seek!

Siamese cats enjoy having a friend to play with.

Glossary

breeds (BREEDS) Breeds are types of animals that are different from other members of its species. Siamese is one of the most popular cat breeds.

Buddhist (BOO-dist) A Buddhist is someone who practices the religion based on the teachings of Guatama Buddha. Buddhist priests treasured their Siamese cats as pets.

climate (KLYE-mit) Climate is the average weather conditions of a place. Siamese cats living in colder climates have denser fur coats.

kink (KINGK) A kink is a short tight twist. Siamese cats used to have a kink in their tails.

mat (MAT) To mat is to become a tangled mess. Siamese coats do not mat.

points (POINTS) Points are distinguishing features. Siamese cats can have four different colors of points.

prey (PRAY) Prey is an animal hunted by another animal for food. Siamese use their strong teeth to catch prey.

stocky (STOK-ee) To be stocky is to be sturdy and thick in build. The first Siamese cats used to be more stocky.

tomcat (TOM-kat) A tomcat is a pet male cat. Tomcat DC was a character in a popular film.

vaccines (vak-SEENS) Vaccines are shots that prevent animals or humans from getting an illness or disease. Siamese cats should get vaccines if they are sick.

veterinarians (vet-ur-uh-NER-ee-uhns) Veterinarians are doctors that treat animals. Veterinarians will take care of a sick Siamese.

vocal (VOH-kuhl) Vocal is to use your voice. Siamese cats are very vocal.

To Learn More

BOOKS

Owen, Ruth. *Siamese*. New York: Rosen Publishing, 2014.

White, Nancy. *Siamese: talk to me!* New York: Bearport Publishing, 2011.

WEB SITES

Visit our Web site for links about Siamese cats:
www.childsworld.com/links

*Note to Parents, Teachers, and Librarians: We routinely verify our Web links to make
sure they are safe and active sites. So encourage your readers to check them out!*

Index